KU-163-369

Emma
the Easter
Fairy

by Daisy Meadows

Join the Rainbow Magic Reading Challenge!

Read the story and collect your fairy points to climb the Reading Rainbow online. Turn to the back of the book for details!

This book is worth 10 points.

9010253570

EAST RIDING
OF YORKSHIRE COUNCIL

Schools Library Service

FICTION
2017

Special thanks to
Tracey West

ORCHARD BOOKS

First published in Great Britain in 2011 by Orchard Books
This edition published in 2016 by The Watts Publishing Group

1 3 5 7 9 10 8 6 4 2

© 2016 Rainbow Magic Limited.
© 2016 HIT Entertainment Limited.
Illustrations © Orchard Books 2011

HIT entertainment

The moral rights of the author and illustrator have been asserted.
All characters and events in this publication, other than those clearly in the public domain,
are fictitious and any resemblance to real persons, living or dead, is purely coincidental.

All rights reserved.
No part of this publication may be reproduced, stored in a retrieval system, or transmitted, in any form
or by any means, without the prior permission in writing of the publisher, nor be otherwise circulated in
any form of binding or cover other than that in which it is published and without a similar condition
including this condition being imposed on the subsequent purchaser.

A CIP catalogue record for this book is available from the British Library.

ISBN 978 1 40834 902 1

Printed in Great Britain

MIX
Paper from
responsible sources
FSC® C104740

The paper and board used in this book are made from wood from responsible sources

Orchard Books
An imprint of Hachette Children's Group
Part of The Watts Publishing Group Limited
Carmelite House, 50 Victoria Embankment, London EC4Y 0DZ

An Hachette UK Company
www.hachette.co.uk
www.hachettechildrens.co.uk

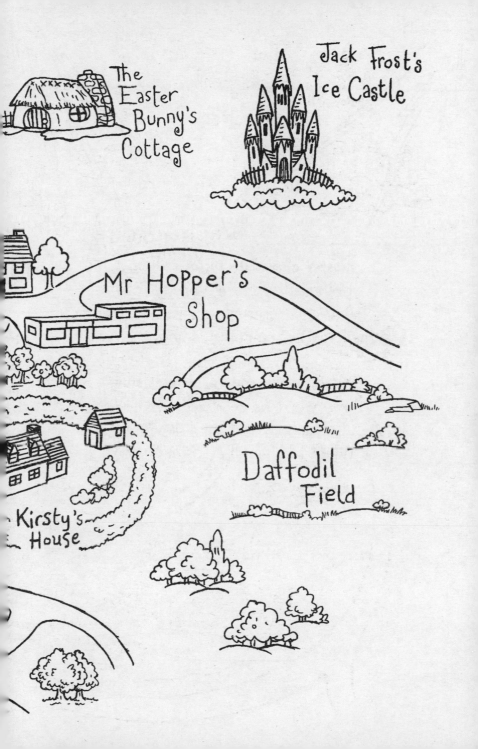

Easter chocolate tastes so sweet,
Coloured eggs are a pretty treat.
And children smile on Easter Day
When the Easter Bunny comes their way.

But I'll make chocolate melt away.
There won't be coloured eggs today.
And nobody will think it's funny,
When I kidnap the Easter Bunny!

The Sweet Treat Disaster

Contents

A Melted Mess!

"We're finally here!" Rachel Walker cried as her dad pulled the car to a stop in the driveway.

Rachel's best friend, Kirsty Tate, ran across the lawn to say hello.

"I'm so glad you're staying with us for the whole Easter weekend!" Kirsty said, as Rachel got out of the car.

"I know," said Rachel. "We get to spend two whole days having fun together!"

The two girls had met on holiday
on Rainspell Island. They were always
excited to have a chance to visit
each other.

"We've got so many fun things
planned," Kirsty said. "We're going to dye
eggs for the big Easter egg hunt, and go
to Strawberry Farm, and—"

"First we have to unpack," Mrs Walker
said with a smile. "Rachel, why don't you
and Kirsty grab the cool box?"

Rachel and Kirsty both picked up the
blue cool box and carried it up the steps
to Kirsty's back door.

"This is heavy!" Kirsty remarked. "What's in it?"

Rachel grinned. "It's a special surprise."

When they entered the kitchen, Rachel's parents were chatting with Mr and Mrs Tate.

"Hello, Rachel. Happy Easter!" said Kirsty's mum.

"What have you got in that big cool box?" asked Kirsty's dad.

"Can I tell them, Mum?" Rachel asked.

Mrs Walker nodded, smiling.

"Mum and I made special Easter chocolates," Rachel said. "We made bunnies, flowers, chicks, and even chocolate eggs. Then we wrapped them in sparkly paper! They look so pretty."

Rachel opened the lid to show them.

"Oh, no!" she gasped.

"What's wrong?"
Kirsty asked.

Inside the cool
box, the chocolates
had melted into one
big, gooey mess! The
sparkly wrappers had
slipped off and fallen
into the sticky chocolate.

"They're all ruined!" Rachel cried.

Mrs Walker looked over Rachel's
shoulder and frowned.

"That's odd," she
said. She felt the
inside of the lid.
"We packed that
cool box with
plenty of ice packs.

14

It still feels chilly inside. The chocolates shouldn't have melted."

Rachel tried not to look too sad, but she couldn't help it.

"But they did melt. And now there's no chocolate for Easter."

"Don't forget about the Easter Bunny," Mrs Tate reminded her. "I'm sure he'll bring you lots of chocolate in your Easter basket."

"He always does," Kirsty said, trying to cheer up her friend.

"I'd better clean this up," said Rachel's mum. "Why don't you girls go outside for a while? It's a beautiful day."

The girls went outside and sat on Kirsty's front porch. Pretty pink and yellow tulips bloomed in the flowerbed there.

"It's strange that the chocolate melted, even though the cool box was still cold," Kirsty said.

Rachel nodded. "I was thinking the same thing," she said. She lowered her voice. "Do you think Jack Frost has something to do with it?"

The girls had a special secret. They were friends with the fairies! Because of that, they knew Jack Frost and his goblins were always causing trouble in Fairyland. Sometimes they played their tricks on the human world, too.

"Maybe," Kirsty replied. "But it's hard to believe there could be goblins around on a nice sunny day like today."

"A beautiful day won't keep the goblins away!" a musical voice cried just then.

One of the pink tulips began to shake.

The petals opened up, and a tiny fairy
flew out! The air shimmered around her
as she flew towards the girls.

"You must be Rachel and Kirsty," said
the fairy, twirling in the air. "I'm Emma
the Easter Fairy!"

Emma wore a pastel yellow dress with a pretty pink sash around the waist. She had polka-dot wellington boots on her feet, and bouncy curls held back with a flowery headband.

"It's nice to meet you," Rachel said.

"Hi, Emma," said Kirsty.

"Happy Easter!"

"I'm afraid there might not be a happy Easter this year," Emma said, perching on Kirsty's shoulder and looking glum. "The Easter Bunny is missing!"

Emma's Story

"Missing!" Rachel exclaimed. "Did Jack Frost kidnap him? It's just the sort of mean thing he would do."

"You're right," frowned Kirsty. "Do you remember the time he stole Santa's sleigh?"

"That's exactly what I thought," Emma said. "But he's getting even sneakier! Let me show you."

Emma waved her wand, and in a burst of sparkles two Easter eggs appeared in midair. Both were painted with pretty flowers. Rachel and Kirsty each took one.

"Look through the pointy end," Emma told them.

Each of the eggs had a small window at one end. The girls looked through them.

"I can see Fairyland!" Rachel exclaimed.

"That's right," Emma said. "And that's my cottage."

Thanks to Emma's fairy magic, they could see inside Emma's red-and-white toadstool cottage. Emma was happily painting Easter eggs with a paintbrush. A white chicken perched on the chair behind her, watching.

"It's my job to add the extra sparkle to Easter," Emma explained. "Every year, my pet chicken, Fluffy, lays three magical eggs. On the first egg, I paint a picture of a chocolate bunny. That egg helps to make Easter chocolate extra yummy."

"Mmm," said Kirsty, licking her lips. "I love Easter chocolate."

"On the second egg, I paint a picture of a colourful Easter egg," Emma told them. "That egg helps make all of the painted Easter eggs bright and beautiful, and stops them going bad."

"So that's why Easter eggs always look so pretty!" Rachel said.

Emma nodded, looking proud. "On the third egg, I paint an Easter basket," the fairy went on. "That's the most important egg of all! It gives the Easter Bunny the extra magical push he needs to deliver all of the Easter baskets in just one night."

The girls held the eggs to their eyes again and watched the story unfold. They saw Emma put the finishing touches on her final painted egg. Then she smiled, gave Fluffy a pat on the head, and flew off.

24

"I wanted to tell the Easter Bunny that I had finished the eggs," Emma said. "But when I got to his cottage, he wasn't there! I looked all over Fairyland, but I couldn't find him."

In the picture, the girls saw Emma flying around Fairyland. Finally she went to the castle to find Queen Titania and King Oberon.

"I told them that the Easter Bunny was missing," Emma explained. "They suspected Jack Frost straightaway, because last year, Jack tried to use a spell to turn all of the Easter eggs rotten. The Easter Bunny stopped him, and Jack Frost has been angry ever since."

"So Jack Frost *must* have kidnapped the Easter Bunny!" said Kirsty.

"Watch and see," Emma said.

In the picture, Emma followed the king and queen as they rushed to Jack Frost's Ice Castle. Jack Frost sat on his icy throne, grinning.

"He told us he had no idea where the Easter Bunny was," Emma said. "He invited the king and queen to search the castle. But the Easter Bunny was nowhere to be found."

"So was Jack Frost telling the truth?" Rachel asked.

"It looked like it," Emma said. "But then I suddenly remembered the three magical eggs in my cottage. I flew back home as quickly as I could to check they were OK."

The picture inside the eggs changed again. Emma flew towards her toadstool cottage. The girls could see Jack Frost's goblins heading towards her house! Emma waved her wand, and silver glitter floated through the air.

The magic glitter trickled inside the

cottage and surrounded the three magical eggs. The eggs disappeared just as the goblins burst through the door. They were safe!

"I sent the eggs here to Wetherbury," Emma said. "I don't know where they ended up, but they should be safe from the goblins."

"But not for long," Rachel pointed out. "The goblins are sure to try to ruin Easter in every way! We need to find the eggs first."

"Not only that," Kirsty added, "but we have to find the Easter Bunny, too!"

Goblins in the Grocer's

"Emma, is that why our Easter chocolates melted?" Rachel asked. "Because the magic eggs are missing?"

Emma nodded. "Yes. And that's not all. The Easter chocolate won't taste nice. The dyed Easter eggs will be ugly and rotten. And worst of all, the Easter Bunny won't be able to visit girls and boys at Easter!"

"That sounds terrible!" Kirsty said.

"It would be, but there's still hope," Emma said with a smile. "Especially now that I have you two girls to help me."

Rachel jumped up. "You said the eggs are somewhere here in Wetherbury. We should start looking straightaway!"

"But eggs are so small," Kirsty said. "How will we ever find them if they could be anywhere in the village?"

Rachel was thoughtful. "Maybe we

should start looking in places where you'd normally find eggs."

"Like the grocery shop!" Kirsty chimed in.

Just then, the girls heard footsteps coming towards the front door.

"Emma, hide!" Rachel whispered.

Poof! Emma vanished, leaving a trail of fairy dust shimmering in the air behind her.

And just in time! A moment later, Mrs Tate and Mrs Walker stepped onto the porch.

"How are you girls getting on?" Mrs Tate asked.

"Fine, Mum," Kirsty said. "We were thinking about going for a walk. Do you need anything from the grocery shop?"

"Actually, I do," her mum replied. "I bought some eggs to paint tonight. But they seem to have gone off already. It's very strange! Mr Hopper always sells nice, fresh eggs."

"Maybe they were a bad batch," Mrs Walker suggested.

Rachel and Kirsty looked at each other. They knew that Emma's missing magic egg was the real reason the eggs had gone off.

"We'll get some more," Kirsty offered.

Mrs Tate gave Kirsty money for the eggs, and the girls set off for the village.

"Wetherbury Village is very nice," Emma said, suddenly fluttering in the air next to them. "All the pretty flowers remind me of Fairyland."

"Thank you," Kirsty said. "Fairyland is beautiful, too."

"But there's still no sign of the Easter Bunny there," Emma said. "I hope we can find him soon!"

As they turned the corner, they walked past the pet shop. The sign on the door said CLOSED FOR EASTER.

Emma suddenly shivered.

"Emma, are you cold?" Rachel asked, concerned.

"No, this is a different kind of shiver," Emma replied. "Fairies can sense when magic is near. It makes us feel tickly all over." She looked around. "I can't see any other fairies nearby, can you?"

Rachel and Kirsty looked everywhere, but they couldn't see any other fairies.

"No," Rachel said. "And that reminds me — you should hide, before someone sees you!"

"Of course!" Emma said, fluttering into the pocket of Rachel's pink dress.

"Make sure you keep your head down," Rachel whispered.

Only she and Kirsty knew about the fairies and their magic, and they had promised to keep them a secret.

A few minutes later, they finally arrived at Mr Hopper's grocery shop. They opened the door, and a blast of cool air hit them.

"*Now* I'm shivering because I'm cold!" Emma called from her hiding place.

Right next to the front door was an Easter display. A big stuffed Easter Bunny sat on a mound of fake grass. He held a basket of colourful plastic eggs. A sign on the display said GET YOUR EASTER TREATS HERE!

A long queue of people were waiting to pay. They were all holding bags of sweets and chocolate, and they didn't look very happy.

Behind the counter, Mr Hopper looked very worried. Two boys in baseball caps were arguing in the aisle full of sweets.

"*I* want the green jellybeans!" one boy yelled.

"No, *I* want the green jellybeans!" shouted the other.

Kirsty spotted her friend Andy waiting
in the queue.

"Andy, why is it so crowded in here?"
she asked him.

"Something's wrong with Mr Hopper's
sweets," Andy replied. "All the chocolate
has melted, even though it's freezing in
here. And other things don't taste right."
He held out an open bag of jellybeans.
"These taste awful! You should try one."

38

Rachel and Kirsty looked at each
other. Eating horrible jellybeans didn't
sound like fun, but they had to see for
themselves.

Kirsty carefully picked out a white
jellybean from the bag. Rachel picked
a blue one.

Kirsty popped the jellybean into her
mouth. Then she made a face. "It tastes of
onions!" she cried.

Rachel stuck out her tongue. "Mine tastes like cheese. *Yuck!*"

"Mum wants me to get my money back," Andy said.

Kirsty sighed. "Poor Mr Hopper!"

Rachel tapped her on the shoulder. "Kirsty, we should find those eggs for your mum." She lowered her voice so only Kirsty could hear. "Maybe we'll find a magic egg there, too."

They waved goodbye to Andy and walked over to the aisle stocked with eggs and milk, where it was quieter.

Emma popped her head out of Rachel's pocket. "We have to find the magic egg that makes Easter sweets and chocolate delicious – and fast!" she said anxiously.

"Let's start looking through these egg boxes," Rachel suggested.

But just then, some loud shouts came
from the sweets aisle. The two fighting
boys were now wrestling over the bag of
green jellybeans. They rolled right past
the girls.

"Give it to me!" one boy cried.

"Never!" replied the other.

The girls jumped back to get out
of their way. Then Rachel noticed
something. Both boys wore baseball caps,
shirts and jeans. But they didn't have any
shoes on their feet...their *green* feet.

"Kirsty, those aren't boys at all!" she
whispered. "They're goblins!"

The Jellybean Trail

The girls hurried to the cereal aisle, where the goblins couldn't see them.

"I should have known!" Kirsty said. "Only goblins would fight over green jellybeans."

"They're here for the same reason we are," Emma piped up. "To find the missing magic eggs!"

"Then we have to find them first," Rachel said.

Kirsty nodded. "And we have to get
those goblins out of here before someone
sees them."

The girls heard more shouting from the
eggs and milk aisle. They peeked around
a shelf and saw three more goblins dressed
as boys, opening up all of the egg boxes!
Eggs spilled and cracked on the floor as
the goblins carelessly rummaged through
them.

"Oh, no! What if one of the magic eggs is in there?" Kirsty asked.

Rachel looked thoughtful. She had an idea! "We know that goblins like green jellybeans. Emma, can you use your magic to make some?"

Emma flew out of Rachel's pocket. "Of course! I'm the Easter Fairy. Making sweet treats is my speciality!"

"Perfect," Rachel said. "If you make a trail of green jellybeans from the goblins to the front door, the goblins will follow them outside."

"That's a great idea!" Kirsty agreed. "Just make sure no one sees you, Emma."

Luckily, the customers in the shop were too upset about their melted chocolate and ruined sweets to notice the goblins. Careful to stay out of sight, Emma flew into the eggs aisle and waved her wand. Green sparkles shot from it. When the sparkles hit the floor, they turned into green jellybeans! Emma made a trail of green jellybeans all the way down the aisle. It didn't take long for the goblins to notice.

"Look – green jellybeans!" one of them cried out.

The two wrestling goblins stopped fighting immediately. The other goblins dropped their egg boxes. All five of them started to race after the jellybeans.

"It's working!" Kirsty cheered quietly.

Emma made a magical trail of jellybeans that led all the way to the front door. The goblins followed the trail, scooping up the jellybeans as they appeared. They shoved and pushed each other to get to them.

Rachel and Kirsty watched the goblins from a safe distance. Once the goblins were outside, the girls would be able to look for the missing magic eggs.

But the goblins stopped before they went through the front door of the shop.

47

"What's happening?" Rachel wondered.
One of the goblins had spotted
Mr Hopper's Easter display. "I think
I see something," he said, squinting.

The goblin stuck his hand inside the
basket of plastic eggs. Then he pulled
out an egg that was glittering with
fairy magic. The egg was white, with a
picture of a
chocolate
bunny
painted
on it.
"I've
found
one of the
silly magical
eggs!" the goblin
howled. "Wait until Jack Frost sees this!"

With that, the goblins cheered and raced through the door.

Rachel and Kirsty dashed to catch up with them. "We can't let them get away!" Kirsty cried.

Help from the Sky

The girls found Emma hovering outside the shop.

"Oh, dear!" she said. "My jellybean trail led those goblins straight to the magic egg. What bad luck!"

"They're heading for the park," Kirsty said, pointing. "We can catch up if we hurry."

The girls ran quickly and nearly caught
up with the goblins. But the goblins kept
going! They ran straight into the woods
at the edge of the park.

"We could lose them in the trees,"
Rachel said, worried.

"But we won't," Emma said. "Stand
still!"

Emma waved her wand and fairy dust
sprinkled out and swirled around the
girls. The whirling cloud of glittering dust
swept them off their feet. The girls could
feel themselves getting smaller!

"We're turning into fairies!" Kirsty cried
happily.

"Now we can all fly around the trees
and catch up with the goblins," Emma
told them.

Rachel set off. "Let's go!"

Rachel was the first to reach the goblin carrying the magic egg. She swooped down and tried to grab it, but the goblin spotted her.

"Hey, it's a fairy!" The goblin scowled. "Hands off my egg!"

The goblin tossed the egg to another goblin. Kirsty flew as fast as she could, hoping to scoop the egg out of the air. But the other goblin jumped up and grabbed it.

"Ha, ha! You can't get it!" the goblin taunted, holding up the egg.

Emma flew down and tried to take the egg from him. But one of his goblin friends warned him. "Behind you!"

The goblin turned and saw Emma just in time. He threw the egg to another one of his friends.

"This is a fun game!" the goblin said with a mean cackle of laughter. "Keep away from the fairies!"

Kirsty flew up to Rachel. "These goblins are too fast!"

At that moment, Emma began to sing a tune. It didn't have any words, but it sounded pretty, almost like a bird singing.

Rachel and Kirsty looked at each other. Why was Emma singing at a time like this?

"Caw! Caw! Caw!"

Five beautiful birds swooped down from the trees, drawn by Emma's song. She had called them to help!

"Friends, please help us get the magic egg back from these goblins!" Emma called out.

The birds dived at the goblin holding the egg. They flapped around his head with their wings.

Startled, the goblin dropped the magic egg. One of the birds broke free and grabbed the egg in its claws before it reached the ground.

"Get those birds!" the goblin cried.

But the birds dived at the other goblins. The goblins were so scared that they forgot all about the magic egg! Instead, they shrieked and ran away.

Giggling, Emma sprinkled fairy dust on Rachel and Kirsty again, and they turned back to human-size.

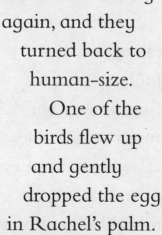

One of the birds flew up and gently dropped the egg in Rachel's palm.

Help from the Sky

"Thank you so much, friends!" Emma
called out.

The birds flew in a circle around the
girls and Emma, tweeting happily. Then
they soared off into the trees.

"We did it!" the girls cheered.

"Yes, we did," Emma said happily. "And
now I've got to get this magic egg back
to Fairyland. I'll give it to the king and
queen so they can keep it safe."

Emma waved her wand and fairy dust
sprinkled over the egg, shrinking it back
to fairy-size. Then Emma took the egg
from Rachel.

"Goodbye, girls — thanks for your help!"
Emma said, blowing them each a kiss.
"I'll see you soon!" Then she vanished.

"At least one magic egg is safe,"
Rachel smiled.

"That's good," agreed Kirsty. "But now, we'd better get back to Mr Hopper's shop and buy those eggs for my mum."

Back at the shop, the girls found one box of eggs that the goblins hadn't broken. They also found a crowd of happy customers.

"Look, my chocolate bunny isn't melted any more," said one man.

Another woman munched on some jellybeans. "And these are delicious!"

"It looks like all the Easter sweets are yummy again," Kirsty smiled.

Rachel grinned. "Maybe we should try some, just to be sure."

That night, the girls nibbled on chocolate chicks while they painted Easter eggs. Mrs Tate gave them six small cups. The girls put a pellet of dye in each cup and added some vinegar. Soon each cup held a different bubbling bright colour: pink, yellow, green, purple, blue and orange.

"It's almost like fairy magic," Kirsty whispered as she dipped an egg into the yellow dye.

"I hope they look nice when they're done," Rachel said, worried. "The magic egg that gives Easter eggs their extra sparkle is still missing."

"And so is the egg that helps the Easter Bunny," Kirsty added.

Kirsty gently put her yellow egg on a paper towel to dry. As she did so, the eggshell started to shake and crack. Emma popped out of the egg and flew up with a giggle!

"I'm sorry I broke your egg," she said. "It's just such a

fun way to get into your world."

"That's OK, we have a lot of eggs!"
Kirsty said. "We're painting them for the
big Easter egg hunt tomorrow at Daffodil
Field. Wetherbury holds one every year on
the day before Easter."

"That sounds like fun," Emma said. She
fluttered her wings and looked nervous.
"But we're so close to Easter, and we still
haven't found the Easter Bunny!"

"We still have a whole day to find him,"
Rachel assured her.

"Yes, and you still have *us* to help you,"
Kirsty reminded her.

Emma brightened. "You're right!
If anyone can find the Easter Bunny,
we can!"

Rotten
Egg Hunt

Contents

A Magical Feeling

"Are you sure it's OK if Mrs Walker and I go out early?" Kirsty's mum asked. "We volunteered to help hide the eggs for the big Easter egg hunt, so we need to get there before everyone else."

It was the morning before Easter. Rachel and Kirsty had stayed up past their bedtime, whispering about all the adventures they'd had the day before.

Now they were finishing the delicious blueberry pancakes Mrs Tate had made for breakfast.

"It's fine, Mum," Kirsty said, smiling. "We'll meet you at Daffodil Field when the Easter egg hunt starts."

That will give us some time to figure out how we're going to find the other two missing eggs, Kirsty thought. *And the Easter Bunny, too!*

Outside, a car horn beeped. Mrs Tate gave each of the girls a quick kiss.

"See you later! I'm sure you'll both find lots of eggs," she said, before hurrying out of the door.

Rachel yawned. "How many eggs do they hide for the egg hunt?" she asked Kirsty.

"It must be hundreds!" Kirsty replied, her eyes shining with excitement. "The entire field is covered with blooming daffodils. The eggs are hidden all over the field."

"That sounds pretty," Rachel said dreamily.

Just then, the air over the table shimmered for a moment.

"I love daffodils!" a voice called
out cheerfully. Emma appeared in the
air, fluttering her wings and grinning.
"They're always in bloom at Easter time."

Rachel waved hello to their fairy friend.
"You should come to the egg hunt," she
suggested.

Kirsty nodded. "You would love it.
Besides, an
Easter egg
hunt would
be a perfect
hiding place
for a
magic egg,
wouldn't it?"

Emma
clapped her
hands together.

"Oh, you're right!" she cried happily.
"Can we go there now?"

Kirsty looked at the clock. "We're not
allowed onto the field until the eggs are
hidden. But if we leave soon, we won't
have to wait for long."

"Then let's go!" Emma said eagerly.
"Tomorrow is Easter Day. Time is
running out!"

The girls quickly washed up their
breakfast dishes, changed out of their
pyjamas, and set off for Daffodil
Field. Their walk took them through
Wetherbury, past the village shops.

Emma started to shiver as they passed
the pet shop. "There's that magical
feeling again," she said, looking around.
Mr Hopper's shop was further along the
street. "I wonder what it could be."

"Yesterday we found the magic egg in the grocery shop after you shivered," Kirsty said. "Maybe there's another one there."

"We could check," Rachel suggested.

"OK, but be on the lookout for Jack Frost's goblins," Emma warned. Then she darted out of sight into Kirsty's pocket.

Things were much quieter in the grocer's shop that morning. There were no

long queues of people making complaints.
The jellybeans and broken eggs had all
been cleaned up. But behind the counter,
Mr Hopper looked sad.

"Is everything OK, Mr Hopper?" Kirsty
asked.

Mr Hopper had grey hair and a round
face. He pushed his glasses up his nose
when he saw Kirsty.

"Oh, it's nothing, dear. Tomorrow
is Easter, after all, and that's a happy
day," he said, trying to smile. "And my
chocolate has stopped melting. But
today, I found that all of the eggs in the
refrigerator were rotten! I had to throw
them away."

Rachel and Kirsty glanced at one
another. They knew why the eggs
were rotten!

Mr Hopper pointed to the refrigerator, which was empty. "It's terrible not to have any eggs for Easter," he went on.

"But I have a new delivery coming in this afternoon. I hope *those* eggs are all right."

"I'm sure they will be," Kirsty assured him.

Mr Hopper patted her on the shoulder. "That's nice of you to say. Is there anything I can get for you?" he asked.

"Not at the moment," Kirsty replied. "We're on our way to Daffodil Field." There were clearly no more magic eggs

at Mr Hopper's shop. There were no eggs
at *all*!

"Have fun, girls," Mr Hopper said with
a smile.

As the girls left
the shop, Emma
flew out of Kirsty's
pocket.

"This is awful,"
Rachel said.
"Those eggs are
going bad because
the magic egg is
missing. We have to find it so all the eggs
are OK again!"

"That's exactly what I was thinking,"
Kirsty said. "Maybe we'll find it at
Daffodil Field?"

"Yes, let's hurry!" said Rachel.

The girls walked quickly to Daffodil
Field. As they got closer, they could hear
the sound of the excited crowd. Parents
and children waited along the edge of the
field for the event to start. The children
clutched colourful Easter baskets.

Rachel gasped at the sight.
Hundreds of daffodils were
in bloom!

The yellow flowers were as bright as the sun and the field was so big that Rachel couldn't even see where it ended.

"It's so pretty!" she exclaimed.

"I'll have to paint a picture of this when I get home," Emma said, peeking out of Kirsty's pocket. "Everyone in Fairyland would love to see it!"

Kirsty's dad started speaking through a
megaphone.

"The Easter
egg hunt will
begin when the
whistle blows.
Try not to step
on the daffodils

as you search. There are plenty of eggs
for everyone!"

"Oh, dear," Emma said, suddenly
looking nervous. "There are so many
children here. What if one of them finds
the magic egg before we do?"

"Don't worry," Rachel said. "We know
what we're looking for."

"Exactly," nodded Kirsty. "I'm sure
we'll spot one of the magic eggs if
it's here."

The girls walked to the starting line and each took a basket.

Tweeeeet! Mr Tate blew his whistle.

"Let the Easter egg hunt begin!" he cried.

Daffodil Disguises

Rachel and Kirsty raced between the rows of daffodils. They spotted many eggs as they ran. Strangely, the eggs weren't brightly coloured. The colours were faded, and some were even brown or grey.

"Yuck!" Rachel exclaimed, stopping to look at a horribly dull egg.

"We need to find the magic egg that helps make all painted Easter eggs fresh and bright," Emma reminded the girls quietly. "Without that egg's magic, the Easter eggs won't be nice." Kirsty stopped and scanned the field of daffodils.

"We're looking for a white egg with a picture painted on it," she said. "That should stand out in this yellow and green field."

Rachel pointed to an area up ahead. "Maybe it's by those big daffodils over there," she suggested.

The girls hurried towards the big
daffodils, and Emma fluttered along
beside them. They were a few
rows away when Emma
suddenly stopped in
midair.

"Wait," she
warned. "I don't
think those are
daffodils. Look!"

The daffodils were
moving! Not only that, they
were talking, too!

"There are so many eggs here! How are
we supposed to find a magic one?" one of
the daffodils grumbled.

"Just keep looking," another daffodil
said crossly. "Jack Frost will be so angry if
we don't find it."

"They're goblins!" Rachel realised.

"We'd better hide," Kirsty whispered, crouching down.

The girls got a closer look at the goblins in disguise. Each goblin wore a hat on his head that looked like a yellow daffodil. Their green bodies and clothes looked like flower stems. And they had a fake green leaf strapped to each arm. There were at least five goblins dressed as daffodils!

The goblins started to become loud and rowdy as they searched for the eggs.

"It's over there!" one yelled.

"No, it's over there!" another one shouted.

The goblins tripped over each other as they scrambled to find the magic eggs.

"*Ow! You pulled my petals!*" a goblin whined.

"We'd better get moving," Rachel said. "We can't let those goblins beat us to the egg this time!"

The girls started looking through the daffodils once more. They hadn't gone far when they heard the sound of a child crying. "Oh, no!" Emma cried. "Someone is in trouble."

A Stinky Problem

The girls hurried towards the sound of the crying child. They found two little girls and a boy standing around a pile of broken eggs. Luckily, there were no goblins around. But something still wasn't right.

Rachel wrinkled her nose. "Those eggs are smelly!"

Kirsty nodded. "They look rotten."

One of the little girls was crying. "These Easter eggs aren't nice. I want my mummy!"

Rachel and Kirsty heard the sound of the goblins getting closer.

"Something smells nice and stinky!" one of the goblins said.

Emma peeked out from her hiding place inside Kirsty's pocket.

"We have to get these children away!" she warned. "Otherwise, they might see the goblins."

Kirsty thought quickly and turned back to the children. "We saw some pretty eggs over there," she said, pointing far away from the goblins.

The sad little girl wiped the tears from her cheeks. "Really?"

Kirsty nodded. "Why don't you go and look?"

The children's faces brightened and they scampered away.

"Well, now we have to find the magic egg *fast!*" Rachel said. "If we don't, the whole Easter egg hunt will be ruined."

Emma flew out of Kirsty's pocket. "I'll have a better view if I fly over the field," she said.

"But then everyone might see you,"
Kirsty reminded her.

Emma thought for a moment, then
grinned. "I have an idea."

She waved her wand in a circle.
Rainbow-coloured sparkles appeared like
tiny fireworks in the air.

Then she called out
in a singsong voice:
*"Help me please,
my butterfly
friends.
The goblins are
up to their evil ends."*

Rachel and Kirsty watched, amazed, as
the air around them filled with beautiful
butterflies! Their wings shimmered in
the sunlight. Some were blue, some were
yellow and some were orange.

Emma laughed and flew up into the middle of the crowd of butterflies. She fluttered her delicate wings. "See? If anyone spots me, they'll think I'm a butterfly!"

"Good thinking!" Rachel said. "We'll keep looking down here while you search from the sky."

Emma and the butterflies flew off across the field.

"Finally, that pesky fairy is gone!" a voice cried out.

The girls froze. The daffodils around them jumped up. Rachel and Kirsty were surrounded by goblins!

"Ha! Our plan worked!" a goblin cried, gesturing to his friends. "We'll stay and keep these girls out of the way. The other goblins will follow that fairy to the magic egg!"

The group of goblins laughed.

Rachel and Kirsty were a little bit
afraid – but only a little bit. They had
outsmarted Jack Frost's goblins before.

"What should we do?" Kirsty whispered
to Rachel.

"We could
run past them,"
Rachel suggested.

"Maybe, but
there are a lot
of them," Kirsty
replied. "They
might catch us."

"Hey! No talking!" a goblin snapped.

Kirsty smiled sweetly. "Sorry. We were
just saying how pretty you all look!"

The goblins frowned.

"Pretty? We're not pretty! We're goblins!"
one of them protested.

"But you look like pretty flowers," Kirsty said.

The goblins grumbled. Rachel smiled at Kirsty. She knew what her friend was trying to do.

"Well, not *all* of you are pretty," Rachel said. She pointed to one of the goblins. "You look scary. In fact, *you* might be the scariest one."

The goblin looked proud. "Of course! I'm the scariest of all!"

The other goblins didn't like that.

"No, *I'm* the scariest!"

"No, it's me!"

"Nobody is scarier than *I* am!"

The goblins started to argue. Soon they were shoving and wrestling each other, just like they had done in the grocery shop.

Rachel nudged Kirsty. "They're distracted. Let's run!"

Egg-citement!

Rachel and Kirsty ran straight past the fighting goblins. The goblins were so busy arguing, they didn't even notice!

"Now we have to find Emma before the other goblins do," Rachel said.

The girls scanned the field. A few rows away, they saw the butterflies hovering over a small daffodil patch.

"Over there!" Kirsty cried.

The girls ran towards the butterflies. They spotted a small group of goblins running from the other direction.

Kirsty tried to run faster. "They're going to beat us there!" she panted.

"Maybe we can stop them," Rachel said.

"How?" Kirsty asked.

Rachel quickly bent down and scooped up an Easter egg from under a daffodil leaf. It looked grey and smelled rotten.

Kirsty did the same. Their baskets were filled with rotten eggs by the time they reached Emma.

Emma turned her head and waved
when she saw them. "I found it!" the fairy
called out. "One of the magic eggs!"

The girls saw a white egg perched in
the centre of a daffodil. The egg had a
picture of a colourful Easter
egg painted on it. It
sparkled with fairy
magic.

But two of the
goblins had already
reached Emma.

"I'll take that!" one of
them said, snatching at the egg.

Rachel nodded at Kirsty. "Now!"

The girls pelted the two goblins with
rotten eggs. The eggs broke as they hit the
goblins, splattering them with smelly goo.

"Oh, no!" one of them yelled.

"Yuck!" shouted the other. "It's slimy and cold. This is even worse than having cold wet feet!"

They ran off, leaving the magic egg inside the flower.

Kirsty hurried to the daffodil and picked up the egg. Emma fluttered down next to her, smiling widely.

"Good work, girls!" she cheered. "You did a great job getting rid of those goblins." Emma turned to the butterflies. "Thank you for your help!"

The butterflies flew away across the field in a blur of beautiful colours.

Kirsty looked down at the egg in her hand. "This is the magic egg that makes Easter eggs beautiful and fresh, isn't it?"

Emma nodded. "Yes! I should get it back to Fairyland quickly, before any more goblins arrive to cause trouble."

The fairy waved her wand over the magic egg. The egg shrank down to its fairy-size. Then it floated up and landed in Emma's palm.

"I'll be back soon," Emma told the girls. "We still have one more magic egg to find."

"And the Easter Bunny, too," Rachel added.

Emma nodded, blowing each girl a kiss. She fluttered her wings, and the air around her sparkled and shimmered.

Then she vanished.

Rainbow Magic

Just then, the three children they'd met earlier came running back to Rachel and Kirsty. They looked angry.

"There you are," said the little girl who had been crying. "You told us there were nice eggs over there. But there weren't any!"

She held out her Easter basket. It was filled with grey and brown eggs.

"They're all yucky!" complained the little boy next to her. He crossed his arms in front of him.

At that moment, a beautiful rainbow appeared over the field. Everyone began to *ooh* and *ahh* as they peered up at the sky. The rainbow colours sparkled over the whole field of daffodils.

Rachel and Kirsty looked at each other.

"Do you think it's fairy magic?" Rachel whispered.

"I think so," Kirsty said, gazing around the field. "Look!"

The grey and brown eggs were changing colour right before their eyes! Now they were bright colours with polka dots and swirly designs.

104

"Your eggs look very nice to me," Kirsty
told the little girl.

The three children looked inside the
Easter basket and gasped.

"They're so pretty!" the girl cried.

The little boy's eyes were wide when
he looked back up at Kirsty. "You must
be magic!"

Kirsty grinned. "It's the magic of
Easter," she said.

"There are pretty eggs all over the field now," Rachel told them. "You should go and find more."

"Hooray!" the children cheered, running off. "We should find some eggs, too," Kirsty said, turning back to Rachel. "Our parents will wonder why we don't have any."

Rachel looked worried. "I hope there are some left for us!"

The girls raced through the field once again. Now that they didn't have to worry about goblins, it was fun looking for the Easter eggs.

Rachel found a purple one with yellow stars tucked under a daffodil. Kirsty found

an orange egg with blue flowers all over
it. Each egg they found was nicer than
the last.

"Emma's Easter magic is amazing!"
Rachel said. "These are the
most beautiful eggs I've
ever seen."

"Me, too!" Kirsty
agreed.

When there
were no more
eggs in the
field, the girls
met up with
their parents.

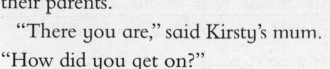

"There you are," said Kirsty's mum.
"How did you get on?"

Kirsty held up her basket. "We found
lots of nice ones!"

Rachel's mum joined them. "Are you sure?" she asked. "Some of the kids were complaining that their eggs were rotten."

Mrs Tate looked around. "That's funny. All of the eggs look fine to me."

Rachel and Kirsty smiled at each other. The magic egg was doing its work! All of the Easter eggs were bright and beautiful again.

"Why don't we go home for lunch?" Mrs Tate asked. "I'll make some egg sandwiches."

"Yum!" the girls said at the same time.

They went home in the Tates' car, past the shops in Wetherbury. Through the grocery shop window, Rachel and Kirsty could see Mr Hopper selling a box of eggs to a customer. He had a happy smile on his face.

"It looks like Mr Hopper's delivery of eggs came in," Kirsty remarked.

"Just in time!" Rachel added.

Then they passed the pet shop. The sign on the door read OPEN.

"I thought the pet shop was closed for Easter," Kirsty said.

"I thought so, too," said Mrs Tate from

the front seat. "Mrs Gilligan went to stay with her daughter, who lives near the beach. Perhaps she got somebody to look after the shop for her."

"Yes, that must be it," said Kirsty, though she didn't sound sure.

When they got home, Kirsty and Rachel sat at the picnic table outside to eat their egg sandwiches.

"I've been thinking about the pet shop," Kirsty began.

Rachel nodded her head eagerly. "Me

too!" she said. "Emma got that magical feeling every time we passed it."

"And it's strange that it was closed for Easter, but now it's open," Kirsty added.

"Strange or *magical*?" Rachel asked, taking a bite of her sandwich.

"Good question," Kirsty said thoughtfully.

"We should go back to the pet shop after lunch," Rachel suggested.

"That's a good idea," Kirsty agreed. "But I think my parents have more Easter plans for us."

"We have to find a way," Rachel said, lowering her voice. "If we don't track down the last missing egg and the Easter Bunny, everyone's Easter plans will be ruined!"

The Easter Bunny Incident

Contents

A Trap

"Mum, what are we doing this afternoon?" Kirsty asked after lunch.

Mrs Tate smiled. "Mr and Mrs Harrison are inviting people to visit Strawberry Farms today," she said. "There were lots of animals born this spring, and we'll be able to meet them."

"Oh, baby animals are so cute!" Rachel exclaimed. "Will there be lambs?"

Kirsty's mum nodded. "And goats, and calves, and baby ducks, too."

Going to the farm sounded like a lot of fun. But Kirsty and Rachel were worried. They had to find the last missing magic egg *and* the Easter Bunny by the end of the day. If they didn't, Easter wouldn't be the same!

"Do Rachel and I have time to go for a walk first?" Kirsty asked.

Mrs Tate looked at the kitchen clock. "We're leaving for the farm at two o'clock, so you have a little bit of time. Go out and enjoy the beautiful day!"

Kirsty nodded to Rachel, and the girls stepped outside into the bright sunshine.

"Now we'll have time to check out the pet shop," Kirsty said.

"I'm sure we'll find something important there," Rachel added. "There must be a reason why Emma got a magical feeling every time we walked past it."

Kirsty looked around.

"Emma? Are you here?"

The pretty little Easter Fairy appeared in a sparkly whirl of fairy dust. "King Oberon and Queen Titania were so happy that we found the second magical egg!" she cried, twirling through the air. "They told me to thank you both."

"We're glad to help," Kirsty said, smiling at her fairy friend. "And we have an idea. We're going back to the pet shop in the village. We think something strange is happening there."

"I'll come with you," Emma told them,
suddenly looking serious.

Emma flew into Kirsty's
pocket and the friends
hurried to the pet shop
together. As they
turned the corner
onto the high street,
Emma suddenly
spoke up.

"Look! Up there,
it's an egg!"

Emma pointed
to a crook in the
branch of a tree
right next to the pet
shop. The girls could
see something sparkly
and white there.

121

Emma was quivering with excitement. "I'll fly up and get it!"

She darted out of Kirsty's pocket, heading straight for the egg. But before she reached it, Emma stopped in midair.

"Oh, no!" she cried.

"Emma, what's wrong?" Kirsty asked.

"I'm stuck!" the little fairy said in dismay. "It's Goblin Gossamer! Their pet spiders weave it. It's very, very sticky. I can't move my wings!"

Rachel shaded her eyes with her hand so she could see better. She spotted Emma up above, struggling, but she couldn't see anything else around the fairy. "I can't see anything," she said, squinting.

"Goblin Gossamer is invisible," Emma told them. "Goblins like to use it to trap fairies. The only way to get out is to sprinkle it with fairy dust."

"Can you use your wand?" Kirsty asked.

"No!" Emma called down. "I can't move my arms."

Rachel was alarmed. How could they possibly help Emma now? Then she looked at the locket hanging around Kirsty's neck. Rachel had a matching one of her own. They were presents from the king and queen of the fairies...and they were filled with magical fairy dust!

"It's a good thing we have some fairy dust," Rachel said.

She opened up her locket and sprinkled some of the fairy dust onto her palm.

Kirsty did the same. Then the two girls blew gently on the fairy dust. It floated into the air, leaving a trail of sparkles behind it.

When the fairy dust swirled around
Emma, the invisible
Goblin
Gossamer
became
visible. It
looked
like a
green
spider web.
After a
moment, the
strands of the web
dissolved, and Emma was free!

"Oh, thank you," Emma cried in relief,
flying down to the girls. "I could have
been trapped there for a long time, if it
wasn't for you!"

"The goblins must have set that trap,"

Rachel guessed. "They were trying to keep you from getting the magic egg back!"

Emma shook her head. "No, that wasn't the magic egg at all. It was a plastic egg sprinkled with glitter."

"Then why did they set a trap?" Rachel wondered. She scratched her head.

Kirsty frowned. "I think they're trying to keep us away from the pet shop."

Just then, the big town clock began to chime. It was two o'clock!

"Oh, no!" Kirsty cried. "We have to get home quickly. We're going to be late for our trip to the farm!"

So Cute!

Kirsty and Rachel ran back to Kirsty's house as quickly as they could.

"Meet us at Strawberry Farm," Kirsty told Emma as they got close.

Emma flew out of Kirsty's pocket. "See you later!" she called, then vanished in a twinkle of light.

Mrs Tate and Mrs Walker were waiting for the girls in the driveway.

"There you are," Kirsty's mum said, opening the car door. "Your dads are going to stay at home and start getting supper ready. We'll take you to the farm."

Kirsty and Rachel climbed into the back of the Tates' car.

"I can't wait to see the baby animals," Rachel said eagerly. "We don't have any farms in Tippington."

"But your town has lots of other fun things to do," Kirsty pointed out.

When they arrived at the farm, the car park was full. The porch of the big white farmhouse was decorated with dangling paper Easter eggs. Next to the house stood a wooden barn. Visitors were walking around a fenced-in field next to the barn. The air smelt of sweet, fresh hay.

Rachel bolted out of the car and ran to see the baby animals.

"Hey, wait for me!" Kirsty called out.

Rachel paused at the fence. "Oh, they're *so* cute!"

In the pen in front of her were three small lambs covered with curly white wool. Next to them were two calves with big, brown eyes.

Grey baby goats munched on hay in another pen.

And in the last pen, fuzzy yellow baby ducks splashed in a small pond.

"They *are* very cute," Kirsty agreed.

Rachel reached through the fence to pet one of the lambs. "Hello, little lamb."

Cock-a-doodle-doo!

A loud crow rang out across the farm.

Rachel jumped. "What was that?" she asked.

"It's a cockerel," Kirsty replied.

"Do they have chickens here?" Rachel asked.

Kirsty nodded. "There's a big coop behind the barn."

Rachel looked thoughtful. After a moment, her eyes lit up. "Kirsty! Where there are chickens..."

"...there are eggs!" Kirsty said, finishing her thought.

The girls looked at each other excitedly.

"Do you think the last missing magic egg could be in the chicken coop?" Rachel whispered.

Kirsty grinned, her eyes shining. "I think it's a good place to look!"

Together, they walked around the big

wooden barn. Through the open door, they saw big cows and lots of sheep.

"Those must be the baby animals' parents," Rachel said.

Kirsty looked around. "I wonder where Emma is?"

They went around the corner of the barn, and found themselves face to face with a small group of lambs.

"I wonder what the lambs are doing out of their pen?" Rachel said. "Do you think they're lost?"

Suddenly, one of the lambs stuck its tongue out. Rachel and Kirsty gasped and stepped back. These weren't baby sheep at all.

They were goblins!

Dancing Chickens

The goblins were wearing fuzzy lamb
costumes, but their green heads were plain
to see.

Rachel put her hands on her hips.
"Move out of our way!" she said bravely.

But the goblins stood in a straight line
in front of them, blocking their path.

"No way!" one of the goblins said.
"We're under strict orders from Jack Frost.

You girls keep messing everything up!"

"*You're* the ones messing everything up!" Kirsty said. "Why can't you just go away and let everyone have a nice Easter?"

The goblins didn't answer. Instead, their eyes grew wide. They looked afraid.

Kirsty and Rachel turned to see Emma flying towards them. Glittering fairy dust drizzled from her wand.

All the big cows and sheep were following the fairy dust!

"*Moo!*" bellowed the cows.

"*Baaaa!*" cried the sheep.

The animals charged past Kirsty and Rachel and stomped towards a nearby field. But the goblins were in their path!

"Run!" one of the goblins cried.

The goblins scrambled in all directions.

Emma flew up to the cows and sheep.
"Thank you, friends," she said
kindly.

"*Mooo*," replied one
of the cows, nodding.
The animals slowly
returned to the barn,
while Emma fluttered
over to Rachel and Kirsty.

"You got here just in time!" Kirsty said
gratefully.

"Yes," Rachel added, nodding. "Thank
you!"

"Those goblins are *such* a pain!" Emma
replied, frowning. "I hope we've got rid of
them for a while."

"Me too," said Kirsty. They had
important things to do! "Rachel and I
were just going to the chicken coop to

look for the missing egg."

Emma fluttered her wings happily. "Oh, what a wonderful idea! Let's go!"

The chicken coop was a large wooden building with wide shelves built along one side. The shelves held rows of small nesting boxes filled with hay, so the chickens could lay their eggs there. Almost every box had a fat, white chicken sitting on it.

"Where are the eggs?" Rachel asked, looking around.

"Underneath the chickens," Kirsty explained. "They sit on the eggs after they lay them. I've helped Mr and Mrs Harrison collect the eggs before. But the chickens don't always like it. Sometimes they make a fuss."

"Then it won't be easy to look for the magic egg, will it?" Rachel asked.

"I know a way," Emma said brightly. "Back home, my pet chicken, Fluffy, loves to dance. This is her favourite song."

Emma began to sing in her musical fairy voice. "*Cluck, cluck, cluck! Cluck, cluck, cluck!*"

The happy chickens all stood up, hopping from one foot to the other.

"That's amazing!" Rachel said, her eyes wide in wonder.

Kirsty ran to the nesting boxes and

looked under one of the chickens. "If there's a magic egg here, we'll find it."

"Wonderful!" Emma exclaimed. "You girls can sing with me, too, if you want."

"*Cluck, cluck, cluck! Cluck, cluck, cluck!*"

Rachel and Kirsty joined in. Now all the chickens were standing up. Some of them moved their heads back and forth to the music.

The girls raced along the rows of boxes, hoping to spot the magic egg. At first, they just saw one plain white egg after another. But then they both noticed something at the same time.

The biggest chicken in the coop was standing over a beautiful, sparkly egg!

Kirsty gingerly reached underneath the chicken and grabbed the egg. It glittered with

fairy magic in her hand and had a
picture of an Easter basket painted on it.

"We did it!" Kirsty cried. "We found the
last magic egg!"

A Pet Shop Surprise

"Oh, this is amazing!" Emma cried
happily. She flew to Kirsty and waved
her wand over the magic egg. It shrunk
down to fairy-size, and Emma scooped
it up. "Once I return this to Fairyland,
the Easter Bunny will have the magic he
needs to deliver baskets to boys and girls
everywhere."

Kirsty frowned. "But we still have to find the Easter Bunny," she reminded Emma.

Emma nodded. "I know. But I'm very hopeful. Thanks to you girls, we've found the three magic eggs. Somehow, I just know we'll find the Easter Bunny."

"We'll do our best," Rachel said.

"I need to take this egg to Fairyland," Emma told them. "But I'll come back and find you as soon as I can."

"And we'll keep looking for the Easter Bunny," Kirsty promised.

Emma waved to them as she vanished in a swirl of twinkling light. "We should try to go back to the pet shop," Kirsty suggested. "I have a feeling about that place."

"Yes," Rachel agreed. "Only this time, we need to keep an eye out for goblin traps!"

The girls walked back to the pens where the baby animals were kept. Mrs Walker and Mrs Tate were feeding grain to the baby goats.

"That tickles!" Rachel's mum said with a laugh. She looked up when she saw the girls. "Are you having fun?"

"Definitely!" Rachel said. "Mum, can

we have a baby lamb at our house?"

"I don't think we have room in our back garden!" Mrs Walker replied.

"But you can always visit us and come back to Strawberry Farm whenever you like," Mrs Tate said.

Mrs Walker brushed the grain crumbs off her hands.

"I need to stop at the grocery shop on the way back," said Mrs Tate.

That gave Kirsty an idea. "Can I show Rachel the pet shop while you're doing that?"

"I don't see why not," her mum replied. "It's just a few doors down."

Kirsty and Rachel looked at each other. They were both thinking the same thing: maybe they would finally find out what was happening in the pet shop!

When they arrived in town, Kirsty
and Rachel waved to their mums and
cautiously walked up to the pet shop.
They saw a sparkly egg sitting on top of
a letterbox nearby.

"Another trap!" Kirsty said. "But it
won't work this time. We've already found
all the missing eggs."

A bell tinkled
as they pushed
open the door
of the pet shop.
Half of the store
was filled with shelves
stocked with pet food, toys and bowls. The
other half was filled with tanks and cages
of pets – hamsters, rabbits and snakes.
A few customers were looking at the
animals, while others shopped for supplies.

Kirsty and Rachel walked through
the aisles.

"Everything seems normal," Rachel
remarked.

"I know," Kirsty said. "I wish Emma was
here. She could tell us if she felt something
magical."

Suddenly, Rachel stopped. "Kirsty,
look!"

Rachel pointed to the glass cage in the
corner that had been set up for rabbits.

It held a small, brown rabbit, a black-and-white rabbit with floppy ears, and a fluffy white rabbit.

The white rabbit was sparkling with fairy magic!

"Do you think it could be the Easter Bunny?" Kirsty whispered.

"May I help you, girls?" a voice behind them asked.

The girls spun around and gasped. They knew that voice!

"Jack Frost! What are you doing here?" Rachel asked bravely.

Jack Frost grinned. He was taller than the goblins, with spiky white hair, and a pointy nose and ears.

"I'm sorry, my name is Mr Jackson," he said. "I'm a friend of Mrs Gilligan's. She asked me to look after the shop while she's away."

"You can't fool us!" Kirsty said, crossing her arms. "We know what you're doing. You've kidnapped the Easter Bunny!"

Jack Frost chuckled coldly. "What lively imaginations you have. Now, if you don't

mind, I must ask you to leave the shop. You're disturbing the customers."

"But we're not—" Rachel began, but Kirsty stopped her.

"Come on, Rachel," she said.

Rachel and Kirsty left the shop.

"Why did we leave?" Rachel asked, confused. "That white bunny in the pen *must* be the Easter Bunny!"

"I know," Kirsty said. "But Jack Frost has got very powerful magic. We can't beat him without Emma's help!"

Happy Easter!

"Here I am!" Emma cried just then, popping into the air in front of them. "The last magic egg is safe in Fairyland."

"Jack Frost is inside the pet shop!" Kirsty told her immediately.

"And we think we found the Easter Bunny," Rachel added. "It looks like a normal white rabbit, but it's all sparkly, as if it might be magical."

Emma clapped her hands together.

"Oh, that's fabulous news! Jack Frost must be using a spell to make the Easter Bunny look like an ordinary rabbit. That's not his true form, of course. We must get him back right away!"

"But Jack Frost is guarding the shop," Kirsty pointed out. "How will we get past him?"

Emma was thoughtful. "We need a distraction of some kind. Then I can fly in, wave my wand over the Easter Bunny, and send him home."

Just then, a group of grumbling goblins slouched along the empty pavement. The goblins looked dirty, and some of them had fake wool from their lamb costumes stuck to their green skin.

"Jack Frost is going to be so angry!" said one goblin.

"We didn't find the magic egg!" wailed another.

"It wasn't our fault! It was those scary cows and sheep," complained the one next to him.

Emma grinned. "Goblins always make a good distraction!" she said brightly. Then she whispered her idea to the girls. "Do you think you can do it?"

Kirsty nodded. "Just watch." She turned to Rachel. "I'm so excited!" she said in a loud voice.

"Me too!" shouted Rachel. "The last magic egg is inside the pet shop."

"But it's in the snake tank," Kirsty replied loudly, biting her lip. "I'm too scared to reach into the tank to get it!"

The goblins raced up to them.

"We're not scared!" one of them bragged.

"We're going to get that magic egg before you do!" taunted another.

The goblins ran into the pet shop, with
the girls and Emma following close
behind. They peeked around a shelf and
watched as the goblins pulled open the
lid of the snake tank. Then they started
picking up the snakes and waving them
in the air.

"Where is it? Where is the magic egg?"
they cried.

The snakes slid out of their hands and
started crawling on the floor.

Jack Frost came around the corner
— and he was furious. "What are you
doing?" he screamed at his goblins. "Put
those snakes down!"

Emma winked at Rachel and Kirsty,
and flew to the rabbit pen. Jack Frost
was so busy shouting that he didn't even
see her.

The girls watched as Emma waved her
magic wand over the
Easter Bunny.

A cloud of
glittering
fairy dust
surrounded
him. The cloud
lifted the
white bunny
up into the air.

But just then Jack Frost noticed what was happening. "No!" he yelled. He ran towards the rabbit pen.

But he was too late.

Poof! The Easter Bunny disappeared.

"That's not fair!" Jack Frost cried, swatting at Emma. But she only giggled, before vanishing as well.

"Jack Frost looks really angry," Rachel remarked.

"We'd better get out of here," Kirsty whispered, edging quietly towards the door.

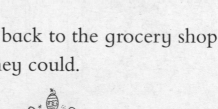

The girls ran back to the grocery shop as quickly as they could.

Back home, Rachel and Kirsty helped to get dinner ready. Afterwards, they played board games with their parents. There was no sign of Emma anywhere!

Later, Kirsty and Rachel snuggled into their beds. They hadn't been able to talk about what had happened that day until bedtime, in case their parents overheard.

"I wonder where Emma is," Kirsty said.

"It's the night before Easter," Rachel reminded her. "I'm sure she's very busy."

Kirsty yawned. "I suppose so. I just hope she got back to Fairyland all right with the Easter Bunny."

"I'm sure she did," Rachel said. "And all three magic eggs are safely back, too."

"That's right," Kirsty agreed. "That means that Easter chocolate will taste delicious, Easter eggs will be fresh and beautiful, and the Easter Bunny will deliver baskets to boys and girls all over the world!"

Kirsty's door opened, and her mum peeked inside.

"Go to sleep, girls," she said. "The Easter Bunny is coming tonight!"

"We know, Mum," Kirsty said, winking at Rachel.

The girls drifted off into a deep sleep. In the morning, they both woke up at the same time. Bright sunlight shone through the window. Outside, the spring birds were singing a happy song.

"The Easter Bunny!" Kirsty and Rachel cried.

They scrambled out of bed and ran downstairs. On the kitchen table were two beautiful Easter baskets. A tag on one said KIRSTY, and the other said RACHEL.

"He came!" Rachel said.

The girls' parents came into the kitchen, yawning.

"I see the Easter Bunny visited last night," Rachel's dad said with a grin.

Kirsty grabbed her basket. "Come on!" she told Rachel. "Let's see what he brought."

The girls took their baskets onto the sunny porch and sat on the steps. They looked through the shiny Easter grass.

Kirsty found a chocolate egg and popped it into her mouth. "Yum!"

Rachel ate a red jellybean. "It tastes like strawberries!"

"And look," Kirsty said, picking up a dyed Easter egg with purple and pink swirls. "It's bright and beautiful!"

Then Kirsty saw the grass in her Easter basket start to move. Out flew the best Easter gift of all — Emma the Easter Fairy!

"Happy Easter!" she cried, hovering in front of the girls.

"Happy Easter, Emma!" the girls said together, grinning.

"King Oberon and Queen Titania are so happy that you helped us find the Easter Bunny," Emma said. "They sent you each a special gift. Look inside your baskets."

The girls eagerly rummaged through the shiny Easter grass. Then they each pulled out a beautiful golden egg.

"Open them up!" Emma said excitedly.

Each egg had a hinge on the back and opened in the middle. A beautiful tune

began to play, and inside, a tiny fairy in a
yellow dress twirled around and around.

"Emma, that's you!" Kirsty realised.

Emma clapped her hands, delighted.
"Aren't they wonderful?"

"She looks just like you," Rachel said.
"Please thank the king and queen for us!"

"Of course!" Emma said. She twirled
around in the air in front of them. "Well,
I have to go now. Today is a busy day!
But thank you again, girls. Have a happy
Easter!"

Rachel and Kirsty smiled at each other.
"We definitely will!"

Now it's time for Kirsty and Rachel to help...

Madison the Magic Show Fairy

Read on for a sneak peek...

Rachel Walker gazed excitedly out of the car window as her mum parked. A short distance away she could see a helter-skelter, a spinning teacups ride, the dodgems, and all sorts of sideshows and stalls. "This is going to be fun!" she said to her best friend, Kirsty Tate, who was sitting next to her in the back seat.

Kirsty grinned. "It looks great," she said, her eyes shining. Kirsty had come to stay at Rachel's house for a whole week during the October half term, and it was lovely to be with Rachel again. The girls always had the best time when they

were together…and the most exciting
fairy adventures, too! They had helped
the fairies in many different ways before,
although their parents and other friends
had no idea about their amazing secret.

"There," Mrs Walker said, switching off
the engine. She turned to smile at the
girls. "Do you want me to come in
with you?"

Rachel shook her head. "We'll be fine,
Mum," she said. "We're meeting Holly
near the helter-skelter in ten minutes, so
we'll go straight there."

"OK," said Mrs Walker. "I'll be back
here at three o'clock to pick you up.
Have a good time."

"We will," Kirsty said politely. "Thanks,
Mrs Walker. See you later."

'Tippington Variety Show' which was

to be held at the end of the week, and Rachel pointed at it. "Mum's got us tickets for that as a treat," she said.

"A variety show…that's one with lots of different kinds of acts on, isn't it?" Kirsty asked.

Rachel nodded. "Yes," she said. "And they're holding auditions for the acts all this week. Today they're auditioning for magicians. Lots of the schools around here have put forward performers, and the best one will get to appear in the Variety Show next Saturday. My friend Holly's been picked from our school to audition, so I said we'd cheer her on…"

Read Madison the Magic Show Fairy to find out what adventures are in store for Kirsty and Rachel!

Meet the
Friendship Fairies

When Jack Frost steals the Friendship Fairies' magical objects, BFFs everywhere are in trouble! Can Rachel and Kirsty help save the magic of friendship?

www.rainbowmagicbooks.co.uk

Calling all parents, carers and teachers!
The Rainbow Magic fairies are here to help
your child enter the magical world of reading.
Whatever reading stage they are at, there's
a Rainbow Magic book for everyone!
Here is Lydia the Reading Fairy's guide to
supporting your child's journey at all levels.

Starting Out

Our Rainbow Magic Beginner Readers are perfect for first-time readers who are just beginning to develop reading skills and confidence. Approved by teachers, they contain a full range of educational levelling, as well as lively full-colour illustrations.

1

Developing Readers

Rainbow Magic Early Readers contain longer stories and wider vocabulary for building stamina and growing confidence. These are adaptations of our most popular Rainbow Magic stories, specially developed for younger readers in conjunction with an Early Years reading consultant, with full-colour illustrations.

2

Going Solo

The Rainbow Magic chapter books – a mixture of series and one-off specials – contain accessible writing to encourage your child to venture into reading independently. These highly collectible and much-loved magical stories inspire a love of reading to last a lifetime.

3

www.rainbowmagicbooks.co.uk

"Rainbow Magic got my daughter reading chapter books. Great sparkly covers, cute fairies and traditional stories full of magic that she found impossible to put down" - Mother of Edie (6 years)

"Florence LOVES the Rainbow Magic books. She really enjoys reading now" Mother of Florence (6 years)

The Rainbow Magic Reading Challenge

Well done, fairy friend – you have completed the book!
This book was worth 10 points.

See how far you have climbed on the **Reading Rainbow**
on the Rainbow Magic website below.

The more books you read, the more points you will get,
and the closer you will be to becoming a Fairy Princess!

How to get your Reading Rainbow
1. Cut out the coin below
2. Go to the Rainbow Magic website
3. Download and print out your poster
4. Add your coin and climb up the Reading Rainbow!

There's all this and lots more at
www.rainbowmagicbooks.co.uk

You'll find activities, competitions, stories, a special
newsletter and complete profiles of all the
Rainbow Magic fairies. Find a fairy with your name!